RAINBOW magic®

The Party Fairies

For Alice and Lara Clerc, with the hope that they will seek out and find lovely fairies in France.

Special thanks to
Marilyn Kaye

ORCHARD BOOKS

First published in Great Britain in 2005 by Orchard Books
This edition published in 2016 by The Watts Publishing Group

1 3 5 7 9 10 8 6 4 2

© 2016 Rainbow Magic Limited.
© 2016 HIT Entertainment Limited.
Illustrations © Georgie Ripper 2005

HiT entertainment

A CIP catalogue record for this book is available from the British Library.

ISBN 978 1 40834 866 6

Printed in Great Britain

MIX
Paper from
responsible sources
FSC® C104740
FSC
www.fsc.org

The paper and board used in this book are made from wood from responsible sources

Orchard Books
An imprint of Hachette Children's Group
Part of The Watts Publishing Group Limited
Carmelite House, 50 Victoria Embankment, London EC4Y 0DZ

An Hachette UK Company
www.hachette.co.uk
www.hachettechildrens.co.uk

Melodie
the Music
Fairy

by Daisy Meadows

illustrated by Georgie Ripper

Join the Rainbow Magic Reading Challenge!

Read the story and collect your fairy points to climb the Reading Rainbow online. Turn to the back of the book for details!

This book is worth 5 points.

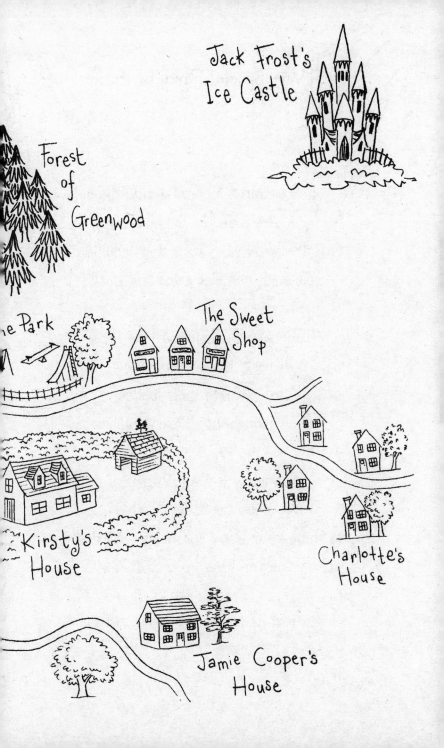

A Very Special Party Invitation

Our gracious King and gentle Queen
Are loved by fairies all.
One thousand years have they ruled well,
Through troubles great and small.

In honour of their glorious reign
A party has been planned,
To celebrate their jubilee
Throughout all Fairyland.

The party is a royal surprise,
We hope they'll be delighted.
So shine your wand and press your dress...
For you have been invited!

RSVP: HRH THE FAIRY GODMOTHER

Contents

Musical Mayhem

"Kirsty, you're a brilliant dancer!" Rachel Walker smiled, clapping her hands as her friend took a bow. Kirsty had just finished practising the ballet steps she would be performing later that evening.

"It will look even better tonight, with the other dancers and the proper costumes," Kirsty replied with a grin.

"And wait till you hear the lovely music."

Rachel was staying with her best friend, Kirsty Tate, for the week. That evening, the girls were going to the village hall for a special occasion – the first anniversary of Kirsty's ballet school.

"It's going to be a great party," Kirsty went on. "My ballet teacher is decorating the hall and organising

some games, and all the parents are bringing food."

"It sounds fun," Rachel agreed. "But if it's a party, then we'll have to be on the lookout for goblins!"

Kirsty nodded. She and Rachel shared a magical secret: they were friends with the fairies! But, right now, there were problems in Fairyland and Kirsty and Rachel had promised to help.

The fairies were planning a surprise celebration for the 1000th jubilee of the Fairy King and Queen. It was meant to be taking place in five days' time, and the Party Fairies were in charge of making it as special as possible using their party bags of magic fairy dust.

But nasty Jack Frost had other plans. Banished to his ice castle by the Fairy King and Queen, he had decided to throw a party of his own on the very same day. Jack Frost knew that whenever a party in the human world went wrong, the Party Fairies would fly to the rescue.

So he had cunningly sent his goblin
servants to spoil as many human parties
as possible, and grab the fairies' party
bags when they flew in to set things
right. Then fairy magic would make his
party spectacular, but the jubilee
celebrations would be ruined!

Suddenly, the girls heard Mrs Tate's
voice. "Time to go, girls!" she called.

Kirsty and Rachel hurried downstairs
to join Kirsty's mum and dad.

Mr Tate held up a cake tin. "I made some cakes for the party," he explained, lifting the lid.

"Fairy cakes!" Rachel laughed with delight. "You couldn't have made anything better."

"Thanks, Dad," Kirsty grinned, tucking the tin under her arm.

Mr Tate drove them all to the village hall. They arrived to find it already full of friends and families who had come to join the celebration.

"The hall looks so different!" Kirsty gasped. Several rows of chairs had been set up to face the stage, just like in a real theatre.

Shiny silver streamers hung from the ceiling, twinkling fairy lights bordered the stage and bunches of silver and white balloons floated above each table of food.

While Mr and Mrs Tate chatted to
other parents, Rachel and Kirsty
arranged the fairy cakes on a plate.
The cakes weren't the
only things that
looked delicious.

"Yum, chocolate
éclairs!" Kirsty
pointed out.
Then she frowned.
"They look almost
too good to be true."

"Maybe we should
test some of these – just
to make sure the food
hasn't been spoiled by
a goblin," Rachel suggested.

Kirsty nodded. She took an éclair and
Rachel ate one of Mr Tate's fairy cakes.

Then the girls smiled at each other – the cakes were delicious, no goblins had been anywhere near this party food.

Just then, the ballet teacher, Miss Kelly, joined them. "Kirsty, it's time for you to go and get ready now," she said. "And you must be Rachel," she added with a smile. "Kirsty said you would be coming."

"Can I help Kirsty and the other girls get ready?" Rachel asked eagerly.

Miss Kelly nodded. "Thank you, Rachel. I could certainly use another pair of hands."

16

Kirsty led the way to the dressing room, which was behind the stage. While the dancers slipped into their tights and tutus, Rachel helped Miss Kelly apply rosy powder to the girls' cheeks and a dab of pink gloss to their lips. Finally, the dancers put on their ballet shoes, tying the pink satin ribbons firmly around their ankles.

There was a feeling of excitement in
the air as the audience took their seats.
Watching from backstage, Rachel
breathed a sigh of relief. The decorations,
the food and the costumes were perfect.
It looked like Jack Frost's goblins hadn't
heard about the ballet-school party.

Miss Kelly walked onto the stage. "Ladies
and gentlemen, I am pleased to present
our very first class of ballerinas, who will
perform for you tonight in honour of our
school's anniversary," she announced.

The audience clapped as Miss Kelly hurried into the wings. Then the curtain rose, and the music began.

With their arms held gracefully over their heads, the dancers ran daintily onto the stage. Having seen Kirsty practise, Rachel knew what was coming next. But she hadn't seen the dance with the costumes and music. She watched in delight – the girls looked as beautiful as fairies in their pretty, gauzy tutus.

But then, suddenly, the music changed. It seemed to speed up and the dancers started to have difficulty staying in time. Although they were dancing on bravely, Rachel could see from Kirsty's face that something was wrong.

She watched in dismay as one or two of the girls stumbled, stubbing their toes on the stage as they tried to pirouette more quickly.

The music was still getting faster and faster, and the tune was now just a squeaky jumble of noise. Rachel glanced across at Miss Kelly.

Red in the face, the teacher was frantically pressing the buttons on the CD-player, one after the other, but it wasn't making any difference. The dancers whirled and spun, quicker and quicker, but it  was impossible for them to keep to the beat. Two dancers bumped into each other, and another tripped over her own feet.

"I can't stop the CD-player!" Miss Kelly gasped. "I don't know what's wrong with it."

But Rachel knew. She was sure that this was the work of one of Jack Frost's goblins!

The Trembling Tambourine

The girls abandoned their performance, and rushed offstage to see what was going on. A couple of the parents came too, to help Miss Kelly with the music. But nobody seemed to know what was wrong with the CD-player.

"This is definitely goblin mischief!" Rachel said to herself. She looked for

Kirsty, but couldn't see her in the crowd of people backstage. "Well, I'm going to find him and stop his tricks!"

Rachel glanced round the village hall, and her heart sank. She could see lots of places where a goblin could hide. Backstage there were trunks and racks of costumes and the big cardboard set from the last pantomime – not to mention two dressing rooms, a music room and a tiny office.

But then, just as Rachel was
wondering where to start her search,
she saw a pile of
musical instruments
stacked in the
wings on the
other side
of the stage.
And one
of them, a
tambourine,
was shaking,
all on its own!

Rachel gulped.
She could see that there was no one
on that side of the stage, and all the
other instruments were still. She knew
the tambourine was too small to hide a
goblin, but what was making it tremble?

Could a goblin have brushed past it
and set it moving, she wondered.
And could the goblin still be lurking
over there?

 As quietly as she could, Rachel slipped
across the stage to the other side. She
crept towards the stack of instruments,
        looking around carefully in case the
            goblin was hiding nearby.
                She wanted to be sure
                    to spot him before
                        he spotted her!
                        But she couldn't
                            see anything
                        suspicious so, with
                    her heart pounding,
                she knelt down beside the
        tinkling tambourine. Very carefully,
Rachel lifted the rim with one finger.

As she did so, a golden glow flooded out from underneath.

Rachel grinned and lifted the tambourine away eagerly. She had already guessed what she would find, and sure enough, tucked away with her face buried in her gauzy skirt, was a tiny, shimmering fairy.

"You're a Party Fairy!" Rachel exclaimed with delight.

The fairy raised her head. She was sobbing so hard that she had been making the tambourine bells jingle.

Tears like tiny diamonds rolled down
her cheeks as she adjusted her little gold
hairband. "That's r-right, I'm Melodie
the Music Fairy," she sniffed sadly. "And
you must be Rachel."

Melodie stood up on tiptoe. She was
wearing a beautiful pink ballet dress, with
black musical notes all around the hem.
Her golden hair was in plaits that swung
as she turned her head.

"Where's Kirsty?" Melodie asked.

"She's not far away," Rachel told her. "But why are you crying?"

Melodie wiped away a last sparkling tear. "I came to fix the music," she explained. "If I had known one of those nasty goblins had made it go wrong, I would have been more careful."

Rachel frowned. "Was a goblin waiting for you?"

"Yes," Melodie wailed. "He grabbed my party bag and ran off with it. Now I can't fix the music for the girls' ballet. And if I don't get my party bag back, there won't be any music for the King and Queen's jubilee party, either!"

Melodie's Mission

Rachel felt very sorry for Melodie. "Don't worry," she said. "Kirsty and I will help you get your party bag back."

Melodie brightened immediately. "Oh, do you mean it?" she cried eagerly.

Rachel smiled. "Of course I do," she replied. "Now let's go and find Kirsty."

Quickly, Melodie picked up her glittering wand and fluttered into the pocket of Rachel's skirt. Then Rachel made her way back towards the people gathered around the CD-player.

Kirsty spotted her friend coming across the stage, and hurried to meet her. "Rachel, I think I know what happened to the music," Kirsty whispered in her ear. "It's goblin trouble!"

Rachel nodded. "Look!" she said,
and held her skirt pocket open so
Kirsty could peek inside.

Melodie waved at
her. "Hello, Kirsty.
I'm Melodie the
Music Fairy,"
she called in her
soft silvery voice.

"Oh, Melodie, I'm so pleased
to see you," Kirsty said gratefully.
"If anyone can help us, you can."

"She came here to fix the music,"
Rachel explained. "But a goblin stole
her party bag."

Kirsty's face fell. "Oh, no!" she
gasped. "We have to get it back
before the goblin escapes and takes it
to Jack Frost!"

Melodie nodded enthusiastically. "But where should we start looking?" she asked.

Rachel thought about this. "There are so many people in the main hall, I don't think he would hang around there," she said. "Let's check the other rooms backstage."

With all the noise and confusion, the

girls were able to slip away easily
without being noticed. They hurried
along the backstage corridor, and ran
into the ladies' dressing room. Rachel
looked in the lockers where the dancers
had left their clothes, while Kirsty
checked the cupboards and rummaged
through the costumes. There was no
sign of a goblin.

Next, they tried the office. Melodie flew out of Rachel's pocket to look under the desk, Rachel peered out of the window, and Kirsty opened all the drawers in the filing cabinet. There were papers and folders everywhere, but no goblin.

The three returned to
the corridor feeling a
little downhearted.

"Do you think
he's already
gone?" Rachel
asked glumly.

Melodie shook her
head, "Not with so many
people about," she replied. "He's hiding
somewhere until the coast is clear."

Suddenly Kirsty frowned. "I can hear
something!" she exclaimed, listening
hard. "Someone's playing the piano."

Now Rachel could hear it too, very
faintly. "Maybe someone is practising
in the music room," she suggested.

"But who would practise the piano
with a party going on?" asked Kirsty.

Rachel listened again. "Well, whoever it is, they certainly need the practice," she said, pulling a face. "It sounds terrible!"

Melodie's face lit up. "Only a goblin could play that badly!" she gasped, and immediately she zoomed off towards the sound. The girls ran after her. As they got closer to the music room, the jangling sound of the piano grew louder.

They found the door ajar, and peeped cautiously into the room. They could hear the terrible music clearly now, and they could even see the piano standing in the middle of the floor. But to their astonishment, there was nobody playing it!

Goblin Discovered

The girls stared at the piano in amazement. Even Melodie looked puzzled. But then Kirsty had an idea. "Maybe the goblin's hiding inside the piano!" she said. "And playing it from there."

"Let's go and look," Rachel suggested.

"No, I'll go," Kirsty replied. "Ballet shoes are soft. If the goblin is in there, he won't hear me coming."

"Good idea," Rachel agreed.
If the goblin was hiding in
the piano, they didn't
want to give him
any warning.

Kirsty slipped
through the open
door and tiptoed
over to the grand
piano. Holding her
breath, she carefully
lifted the lid and
peeked inside.

And there he was – a
nasty-looking goblin, laughing
gleefully and running up and down
the piano strings, with Melodie's party
bag swinging from one knobbly hand.

As he pranced, he sang to
himself in a croaky voice:
"I've got the party
bag, I'm such a
smarty. I'll take it
to Jack Frost,
and he'll throw
a party!"
Ever so gently,
Kirsty lowered
the piano lid.
Then she turned
to the door
and nodded
at Rachel and Melodie.
"What do we do now?"
Rachel whispered to Melodie.
"How are we going to get
your party bag back?"

Melodie frowned thoughtfully, as Rachel looked around the room. There was a set of drums not far from the grand piano, and on one of the drums lay a pair of cymbals. This gave Rachel a clever idea. "See those cymbals?" she said, pointing them out to Melodie. "Do you think you could lift one?"

"I think so," Melodie replied, looking at Rachel curiously.

"Great! I'll take the other one," Rachel said.

"But how will you get there to pick it up?" Melodie asked. "If you walk across the room, the goblin might hear you."

"Not if I'm a fairy…" Rachel smiled.

Melodie nodded and waved her wand. A shower of glittering fairy dust floated down around Rachel and she felt herself shrinking. By the time the sparkling dust had settled, Rachel was as tiny as Melodie herself. She fluttered her wings happily and flew around in a little circle. Then she set off across the music room, with Melodie close behind.

The cymbals were heavy. Melodie
and Rachel both had
to struggle to lift
them, but at last
they managed it.

Quickly, they
flew over to
Kirsty, who had
been watching them in
bewilderment. Rachel whispered in
Kirsty's ear so the goblin wouldn't hear.

"When I wink, open the lid of the piano," she said.

Kirsty nodded, wondering what Rachel was planning.

Rachel and Melodie held up the cymbals and hovered in the air, face to face. Then Rachel winked at Kirsty who immediately lifted the piano lid. At the very same moment, Rachel and Melodie rushed towards each other. And with a crash that shook the room, the cymbals clashed together right above the goblin's head!

A New Problem

The goblin let out a loud scream, clapped his hands over his ears and dropped Melodie's party bag. "Oh, what a dreadful noise!" he shrieked in surprise. "My poor head hurts!" And he leapt out of the piano and ran from the room at top speed.

Rachel smiled to herself. The cymbals had made a deafening noise, she thought, but at least she and Melodie had been ready for it. She heard a smaller crash, and looked round to see that Melodie had dropped her cymbal and swooped into the piano to snatch up her party bag.

"Ooh, that was fun!" Melodie exclaimed. "The goblin escaped, but I've got my party bag and that's all that matters." She opened the bag and peeped inside. As she did so, some glittering, golden musical notes drifted out. "And it's still full of magic fairy dust," she declared happily.

At that moment, Kirsty heard footsteps in the corridor outside. "Someone's coming," she whispered. "Quick, you two, hide in the piano!"

Rachel dropped her cymbal with a clatter and flew to join Melodie inside the piano. Kirsty let the lid down quickly. She was just in time. The door to the room swung open, and Miss Kelly came in. "Hello, Kirsty, are you all right?" she asked anxiously. "Whatever was all that noise?"

Kirsty had to think very quickly.

"Er, I thought that there, um, might be another CD-player in this room," she explained. "I was looking for it when I knocked over the cymbals."

Miss Kelly laughed. "Well, we need you on stage now. I think we'll be able to start the ballet again in a minute. Melissa's dad is an electrician, and he's fixing the CD-player."

Kirsty frowned. Could a human electrician fix a machine that was broken by a goblin? She had a feeling that only fairy magic would get that CD-player working again. And she  knew just who could help. But Melodie was stuck inside the piano with Rachel!

"I'll come in a moment, Miss Kelly," Kirsty said, thinking fast. "Some sequins fell off my costume. I just need to find them first."

"Your costume looks fine," the ballet teacher told her briskly. "A sequin or two makes no difference. Besides, there's no time to sew them back on, and we don't want to keep our audience waiting any longer."

Kirsty had no choice. Reluctantly, she followed Miss Kelly out of the music room, leaving Rachel and Melodie trapped inside the piano.

The Show Must Go On!

"Oh, no!" Rachel cried after Kirsty and Miss Kelly had gone. "Who knows how long we're going to be stuck in here now?"

Melodie laughed, a tinkling musical sound. "Don't worry, Rachel," she said. And with a wave of her magic wand, the piano lid flew open in a

shower of sparkling fairy magic.

Rachel and Melodie flew out. As soon as Rachel reached the ground, Melodie waved her wand again and turned Rachel back to her normal size. Then, clutching her party bag tightly, Melodie hid herself in Rachel's pocket. "We can save the party now," she said happily. "Let's go!"

As Rachel hurried out of the music room, she noticed that the squeaky, speeded-up music had stopped. She wondered if the spell had been broken when the goblin ran away. Or maybe Melissa's dad had fixed the CD-player somehow.

When she reached the stage, however, she saw a large group of people still gathered around the machine. Peering through the crowd, Rachel caught a glimpse of Melissa's dad with a screwdriver in one hand and a pair of pliers in the other. Miss Kelly and Kirsty were by his side.

"What's happening?" Melodie hissed from Rachel's pocket.

"I think Melissa's dad took the CD-player apart," Rachel whispered.

"There are bits of metal and plastic all over the floor."

"Is he going to put it back together now?" Melodie wanted to know.

"I think so," Rachel murmured. She edged a little closer.

"I'm terribly sorry," the man was saying to Miss Kelly. "I've repaired CD-players before, but I've never seen anything like this. I don't think I can fix it."

"Do you think *you* can fix it?" Rachel whispered to Melodie.

"Yes, I'm sure I can – with fairy magic," Melodie answered. She peeped out of Rachel's pocket and her face fell. "But not with all these people around," she added. "Someone would see me sprinkling fairy dust over the machine."

"Maybe I can get everyone to move away," Rachel said thoughtfully. But though she racked her brains, she couldn't think of anything that would make the people leave the CD-player.

She looked round, hoping that a
brilliant notion would pop into her
head. And then she remembered the
musical instruments in the wings on the
other side of the stage, where she had
first found Melodie.

They couldn't be seen from the
CD-player, but when Rachel slipped
across to the pile of instruments, she
was pleased to see that there was
nobody else about.

Gently, she lifted the little fairy out of her pocket. "Look," she said softly. "I've got an idea. Can you do anything with these musical instruments instead?"

Melodie smiled and clapped her hands.

"Yes, I can!" she exclaimed. "Is anyone looking?"

"No, we're out of sight round here," Rachel told her.

Quickly, Melodie fluttered over to the instruments and perched lightly on the violin. She took a handful of glittering musical notes from her party bag, and carefully sprinkled them over the violin's strings.

Then she flitted from instrument to instrument, throwing a few sparkling notes over each one. Finally, she waved her wand with an expert flourish.

At once, the bow that had been lying next to the violin floated into the air and began stroking the violin's strings.

The flute hovered, quivering, as soft, sweet sounds poured from it, while the strings of a harp were plucked by invisible fingers. Rachel heard the deep, low notes of a horn and watched in amazement as all the instruments began to play themselves.

From across the stage, Rachel heard Miss Kelly exclaim in surprise. "That's our ballet music!" she cried. "Where is it coming from?"

Rachel ran back to the group. "I found another CD-player," she told the ballet teacher. She caught Kirsty's eye and smiled. Rachel didn't have to tell her friend that there was fairy magic at work!

"Quickly, dancers take your places,"
Miss Kelly called. As the girls rushed
onto the stage, the audience moved
back to their seats.

Miss Kelly turned
to Rachel. "Could
you start the
music from
the beginning
again, please?"
she asked.

Rachel bit her lip.
She wasn't sure that
she could. What if Melodie had already
gone back to Fairyland? Anxiously,
she hurried back to the instruments,
and then she smiled with relief. She
should have known that Melodie
wouldn't leave without saying goodbye.

The fairy was still there, dancing around to the music, her white dress swirling around her.

"Can you start the music from the beginning?" Rachel asked her.

Melodie's wand fluttered and she threw a few more glittering musical notes into the air. The music stopped for an instant, and then began all over again.

As Kirsty and the others began to dance, Rachel and Melodie watched the performance from the wings. "Oh, it's lovely!" Melodie exclaimed, copying the dancers' graceful arm movements.

"Just like it should be," Rachel agreed.

The ballet went perfectly, and at the end the audience applauded wildly. The girls curtseyed, left the stage and went to join their proud parents. Except for Kirsty, who rushed over to the side of the stage.

"Thank you, Melodie," she said gratefully. "You saved our party."

"No, thank you," Melodie beamed. "Without you, there would be no music at the King and Queen's jubilee. Please keep an eye out for any more of Jack Frost's goblins."

"We will," Rachel and Kirsty promised together.

Melodie beamed. "Good luck," she said, and with a wave of her wand and a shower of twinkling lights, the fairy flew away.

Smiling happily, Rachel and Kirsty made their way to the hall to enjoy the rest of the party.

"I hope we meet more Party Fairies," Rachel said.

"Oh, I'm sure we will," replied Kirsty, and then she smiled. "As long as we keep going to parties!" she added.

**Now Rachel
and Kirsty must help...**

Grace the Glitter Fairy

Read on for a sneak peek...

"Isn't it a beautiful day?" Kirsty Tate
said happily, looking up at the deep
blue sky. "I'm so glad you're staying
here for a whole week, Rachel."

Kirsty was sitting on the grass in
the Tates' back garden, making a daisy
chain with her best friend, Rachel Walker.
Pearl, Kirsty's black and white kitten,
was snoozing in a patch of sunshine
in the middle of the path.

"You know, Rachel," Kirsty went on,
picking another daisy. "This is the perfect
day for—"

"A party!" Rachel broke in, knowing

exactly what Kirsty was going to say.

Kirsty nodded, a frown on her face. "Let's hope horrid Jack Frost's goblins don't spoil someone's special day."

"The Party Fairies will do their best to stop them," Rachel replied in a determined voice. "And so will we."

Rachel and Kirsty had a wonderful secret which no one else in the whole human world knew about. They were best friends with the fairies! So far, the girls had helped the Rainbow Fairies and the Weather Fairies against Jack Frost's evil spells. Now it was the turn of the Party Fairies.

"Isn't it just like mean old Jack Frost to want to spoil everyone's fun?" said Kirsty. "He can't stop causing trouble, even though he's been banished to his ice castle."

"If he hadn't been such a pest, he could have come to the surprise party for the

Fairy King and Queen's 1000th jubilee," Rachel pointed out.

The girls had been invited to the Fairyland party themselves, and they had been very excited about it – until they found out that Jack Frost was determined to have a party of his own. His goblins were causing trouble at human parties, so that the Party Fairies would appear to put things right. Then the goblins would try to steal the fairies' magic party bags for Jack Frost to use at his party.

"Well, we managed to keep Cherry the Cake Fairy and Melodie the Music Fairy's party bags safe," Kirsty said, adding another daisy to her chain. "We'll just have to keep our eyes open."

"And our ears," added Rachel.

Suddenly, there was a scrabbling noise behind the hedge. "OW!" someone muttered. "That hurt."

"Who was that?" gasped Rachel. "Do you think it was a goblin?"

Kirsty grinned and shook her head. "It's OK," she said. "It sounds like Mr Cooper, our next-door neighbour."

At that moment, Mr Cooper popped his head over the hedge. He was a tall, thin man with a cheerful smile. "Sorry, Kirsty," he said, "did I startle you? I pricked my finger on the rosebush." He held up a small parcel wrapped in shiny blue paper. "I'm trying to hide these presents around the garden for the treasure hunt this afternoon."

"Treasure hunt?" repeated Rachel, looking puzzled.

Mr Cooper nodded. "Yes, it's my son Jamie's birthday today," he replied. "He's five and we're having a party."

A party! Rachel and Kirsty glanced at each other in excitement.

"We've got ten children coming," Mr Cooper went on. "And we've hired a clown called Mr Chuckles. Jamie is really excited." He smiled and shook his head. "It's going to be a lot of hard work, though..."

Read Grace the Glitter Fairy
to find out what adventures are in store for Kirsty and Rachel!

Meet the
Party Fairies

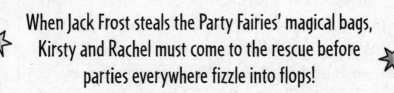

When Jack Frost steals the Party Fairies' magical bags,
Kirsty and Rachel must come to the rescue before
parties everywhere fizzle into flops!

www.rainbowmagicbooks.co.uk

Calling all parents, carers and teachers!
The Rainbow Magic fairies are here to help
your child enter the magical world of reading.
Whatever reading stage they are at, there's
a Rainbow Magic book for everyone!
Here is Lydia the Reading Fairy's guide to
supporting your child's journey at all levels.

Starting Out

1 Our Rainbow Magic Beginner Readers are perfect for first-time readers who are just beginning to develop reading skills and confidence. Approved by teachers, they contain a full range of educational levelling, as well as lively full-colour illustrations.

Developing Readers

2 Rainbow Magic Early Readers contain longer stories and wider vocabulary for building stamina and growing confidence. These are adaptations of our most popular Rainbow Magic stories, specially developed for younger readers in conjunction with an Early Years reading consultant, with full-colour illustrations.

Going Solo

3 The Rainbow Magic chapter books – a mixture of series and one-off specials – contain accessible writing to encourage your child to venture into reading independently. These highly collectible and much-loved magical stories inspire a love of reading to last a lifetime.

www.rainbowmagicbooks.co.uk

"Rainbow Magic got my daughter reading chapter books. Great sparkly covers, cute fairies and traditional stories full of magic that she found impossible to put down" - Mother of Edie (6 years)

"Florence LOVES the Rainbow Magic books. She really enjoys reading now" Mother of Florence (6 years)

The Rainbow Magic Reading Challenge

Well done, fairy friend – you have completed the book!
This book was worth 5 points.

See how far you have climbed on the **Reading Rainbow**
on the Rainbow Magic website below.

The more books you read, the more points you will get,
and the closer you will be to becoming a Fairy Princess!

How to get your Reading Rainbow
1. Cut out the coin below
2. Go to the Rainbow Magic website
3. Download and print out your poster
4. Add your coin and climb up the Reading Rainbow!

There's all this and lots more at
www.rainbowmagicbooks.co.uk

You'll find activities, competitions, stories, a special
newsletter and complete profiles of all the
Rainbow Magic fairies. Find a fairy with your name!